Time Shattered

Copyright Notice

Copyright © 2020 Lawrence Lockett

All rights reserved. No part of this book may be reproduced in any form on by an electronic or mechanical means, including information storage and retrieval systems, without permission in writing from the publisher, except by a reviewer who may quote brief passages in a review.

This is a work of fiction. Names, characters, places, and incidents either are the product of the author's imagination or are used fictitiously. Any resemblance to actual persons, living or dead, events, or locales is entirely coincidental.

Acknowledgements

I would like to thank my editor Charlie Wilson for her help improving my writing.

And thanks to Nik at Book Beaver for working with me to create the cover.

Chapter 1: Facing the End

Around the year 2050, the scientific community unanimously agreed that humanity had damaged the world beyond the point where it could be repaired. It was widely known for decades that global warming and climate change were facts, and that if people didn't change their way of living, one day the Earth would reach a point where it would no longer sustain our race. As the facts became more widely known, the changes easier to see and the time more pressing, action groups formed to try to stop this path towards self-destruction. These groups grew in number, and they arranged marches and protests to draw attention to the approaching disaster, but this didn't have the desired effect. World leaders acknowledged the issue and said that action would be taken, but the status quo continued. Most of the world's population didn't make the changes that were needed, and eventually it was too late to stop climate change and avert the extinction of humanity.

Knowing the facts as they were, people desperately sought alternative solutions for the survival of the human race. Plenty of ideas were discussed. Like other periods in history, some considered bunkers to be the way to survive. If they had enough food and supplies, they could lock themselves away in a bunker or safe refuge until these times had passed. Another idea was to build ships, leave Earth and head for the stars, in the hope of finding a world to settle upon in our vast galaxy. Many variations of the space survival idea were considered, but the reality was that these plans weren't realistic given the current technological level. So many options were considered, but nothing was plausible for anything but the smallest percentage of the world's population.

With the sense of impending doom, many cities and towns in countries all over the world found it challenging to keep law and order. Some people considered it hopeless and thought that it didn't matter what they did, as they probably wouldn't live long enough to face the consequences of their actions. Pockets of chaos sprang up. The police and armed forces were able to restore order, but not without a great loss of life.

Not everyone across the world had given up hope, however. Some of the greatest scientists of the age were working hard on a project called Salvation. This group had studied all the proposed solutions and found that they simply weren't viable. They had an alternative in mind, but it was at the furthest reaches of scientific possibility. Given enough time, nature would repair the damage done by humanity and the Earth would be life-sustaining again. So, they thought, what if we could skip over the years between the present and that time? Those working on Project Salvation had come together shortly after 2050 and had been working for years on developing time travel. Unsurprisingly, there was no shortage of support and finance from the many countries and individuals who knew of the project. The intention was to build a device which would open a doorway through time and into the future, where – or in fact when – life could continue.

Every available resource was put into this project. Not only did they need to find a way to travel through time, but they also needed to choose the time to which they travelled. Granted, travelling far enough into the past could achieve the same results. However, there would be no way of knowing whether they would create a time paradox or worse, so it was far too risky to attempt.

Over the years that followed, the project experienced failure after failure, but with each one they learned something that took them one step closer to success.

Chapter 2: The Unexpected Result

After years of working towards making time travel possible, the team believed that today could be the day of the breakthrough, when they would finally open the doorway to the future. For Isaac, this would be the culmination of his life's work, as he had been working on Project Salvation since its inception. Isaac wouldn't take the credit if today was a success, however; he was one member of a team and it was the entire team that would be responsible for the success.

Isaac stood at the controls as the power built up. It took a great deal of energy to attempt to open a doorway. He was aware of the people around him, busy with their responsibilities. Each person was a cog in a machine, an essential part of making this dream a reality. The blast doors had been raised; there was only reinforced glass between him and the room where the great machine stood. It would direct the stored energy in a controlled, focused burst to open a temporal rift. Through this rift they would send drones to establish whether they had indeed opened a door through time and to confirm that it was the right time.

The energy had built up to the optimal level and Isaac initiated the beam, his colleagues carefully modulating the machine's output for the desired result. As he looked down, Isaac saw the bright-blue beam traversing the large room to hit a point towards the end – not a wall or obstruction, but a point in the middle of the air. A blue sphere was forming at the focal point of the energy beam, and this sphere was growing. *It's working,* he thought. If it continued as predicted, then the sphere would expand further until it became their doorway.

But something was going wrong – the energy was beginning to arc out like bolts of lightning. Isaac spoke into the microphone:

"Evacuate now!"

Those in the machine room quickly moved back towards the door and exited. Isaac hit the blast door release and the barrier dropped almost instantly in front of the control room. Isaac and the others turned their attention to the monitors above them, which were displaying camera feeds of all that was happening. The temporal energy didn't appear to be growing in the centre of the sphere, but continued to arc out.

The energy in the room started to affect the equipment, so the monitor images became less clear. But it didn't matter: the test was almost complete. At the point when they expected the doorway to form and open, they instead saw an explosion of energy in all directions.

The test was a disappointing failure, but at least nobody had been injured or killed. They would need to make the equipment and area safe, and then it would be time to review the data. They soon found that the electromagnetic energy had damaged some equipment and a few things had gone offline. First on the list was to fix and replace the damaged equipment. They got to work.

It took some time for them to discover that not all of the technical issues were related to damaged equipment. There was no internet connection, the landlines were dead and mobile phones were displaying 'No Service' messages. Isaac and others began to suspect something was awry. Why had no one enquired about the results of the test? The team would have expected a visit after a few hours if they couldn't be reached by normal means.

The research facility had been built in a location away from the general population for safety reasons, so there was nobody in the immediate area to answer their questions. Isaac told the team to carry on as usual while he drove to the closest village, a few miles away, to see if he could get answers to the questions that were preying on his mind.

In the village, Isaac didn't see evidence of anything unusual. But once he stopped and talked to some residents, he soon discovered that things weren't normal here either. Nobody was able to contact anyone outside of the local area, and a man claimed that when he tried to drive to the next closest town, he encountered something he could only describe as a wall of blue light. The residents had chosen to wait for help and news rather than investigating or trying to pass through this mysterious phenomenon.

Isaac asked where this wall of light was located. He explained that he was a scientist and that he would investigate this new oddity with his team. Until they knew more, he asked that everyone stay away from the wall, and he promised to return with answers as soon as he had any.

Isaac returned to the research facility and called the team together to share what he had been told by the residents of the village. They agreed that the description of the blue light matched the temporal energy that was released from their experiment, and that they must send a team to investigate.

Chapter 3: Analysing the Mystery

Given that nobody knew what this wall of energy was, Isaac took a team of skilled individuals with him. The team comprised people from different fields of expertise who had come from all over the world to work together on Project Salvation. Isaac was one of the lead scientists, along with Jessica, from the Far East, and Stephen, from America. Adhira was a skilled doctor from India; Laura, from the Netherlands, was a good medic and more; and Thomas, from Canada, was a soldier.

After doing some surveys, they discovered that this wall of light wasn't a singular phenomenon. The team did not know yet how many walls existed, however they found another north of the first wall. It was understandable why this one had been discovered first by the local residents, though: it was the closest and intersected with a main road. A visible difference in the light could be seen in certain places. There were very bright spots, almost white, where it appeared two energy walls connected. The team decided to focus on the closest wall; then they could move on to the others at a later point if needed.

Once the team reached the wall, they began setting up their equipment. Isaac, Jessica and Stephen prepared to test the energy of the wall. Adhira and Laura set up their medical equipment and got organised in case they were needed. Thomas walked around the area to make sure the place was as safe as possible.

First, the scientists tested for any energy coming from the wall. At the beginning of the project, they had experienced side effects from unstable temporal energy and found that those exposed to it could grow much older or younger. The tests confirmed that the wall wasn't radiating any energy, so the risk of side effects was minimal. The energy level of the wall stayed consistent during their instrument scans.

The next stage was to see how the energy would affect an object. The tests would be conducted from a safe distance and by automation. First, the team used a robot with an arm to put a piece of metal very close to the wall of light, and then reviewed the results. Having seen no definable change in the metal fragment, they moved on to the next test, which was to insert the metal into the wall of light itself. The team observed a change in the light around the area where the metal was inserted, but once removed, the wall returned to normal. Again, the metal did not appear to have changed in any way.

For the next phase of their investigation, they would use a living organism. They chose a plant with flowers, so that any aging would be visible. As with the first test on the metal, they began by getting the plant as close as possible to the energy wall without making physical contact. They held the plant close to the wall for some time, waiting to see if the flowers changed, but nothing happened. They brought the plant back to examine it and found no noticeable change.

Next, they put the plant in direct contact with the energy wall. As with the piece of metal, the light shimmered as soon as the barrier was broken. Unfortunately, it was hard to see the plant once it was immersed in the bright-blue light. After an hour or so, they used the robot to retrieve the plant for study. They found no evidence that the plant had been affected by the temporal energy.

At this stage, Jessica suggested that the latest experiment may not have been the failure that they had originally thought.

"What if we've created a stable doorway through time, just not where we'd intended it to form?"

Isaac and Stephen considered this idea for a moment. So far, the testing did support the hypothesis. Objects and living organisms were able to enter the wall with no side effects and this was similar to what they were trying to create.

"The evidence does support your theory. The best way for us to prove the theory is to insert a camera into the barrier and find out what's on the other side," said Isaac.

Stephen wouldn't have suggested such a bold step at this stage, but Isaac often pushed the limits. He wouldn't do anything unsafe, but he'd become a scientist to see what was possible and to advance human knowledge and understanding to a higher level.

After some discussion, the three scientists agreed that the risk was minimal and warranted. The camera was set to record, and then mounted on the arm of the robot and inserted as far into the energy wall as possible.

After a few minutes, the camera was pulled back out and they could examine the footage.

The camera had recorded and the data was intact. When they played the file, they saw the English countryside. This was to be expected: the research facility was in a rural area, miles from the nearest small towns. Early indications were positive, but there wasn't much to see in the footage but the landscape. They returned the camera and left it recording, hoping to film animals or people. Then they could confirm that life (outside of plants) was being supported on the other side and get an idea of the time period.

These tests had taken days, and the residents of the local village had become more concerned as time passed. A group of villagers came to the research camp to ask Isaac for answers. Thomas greeted them as they approached. He didn't want anyone doing something stupid, so he escorted the visitors to see Isaac, Jessica and Stephen.

"You promised us answers, but it's been days and... nothing," said Michael, the villagers' spokesperson. "Plus, we still haven't heard from anyone outside of the local area. What's going on?"

Isaac responded, "We understand your concern, but it's taking time to get answers safely. As soon as we have something definitive, we'll share the information with you."

Having reassured Michael and the other villagers that they were doing all they could, the team returned to their work. After a few more tests with the camera, they had evidence that the place beyond the wall could support life. The camera had recorded birds and various mammals. Now, they had at least an idea of the time period, and it certainly wasn't thousands or millions of years from the present.

Communication signals like radio didn't pass through the energy field, so devices such as drones weren't useful – they would go through the energy field without issue, but then lose contact with the controller and so automatically return. The team had reached a point where they couldn't achieve more without human trials.

Chapter 4: A Peek on the Other Side

The group discussed at length how to proceed next. Although all the tests indicated the energy field would have no negative effects on a human being, nothing was certain until somebody entered it. The question was, who would be the one to take the risk? Isaac, Jessica and Stephen were responsible for the current situation following the Project Salvation test, so they felt that one of them should be first to make contact. Stephen volunteered. Although he had made his contribution to the project, Isaac and Jessica had offered far more. If anything went wrong, then Isaac and Jessica had the greatest chance of fixing it. And so the decision was made. This didn't mean Stephen was enthusiastic – in fact, he was a risk-averse person – but he knew that he needed to do this.

They would proceed in much the same manner as in the earlier tests, beginning with Stephen getting as close to the energy wall as possible without coming into contact with it. Adhira attached a heart rate and other vital signs monitors to record any changes in his condition, so that they could pull Stephen back if needed.

As Stephen approached, his heart rate increased, but this could be attributed to a little anxiety of the unknown. He stopped one step away from entering the phenomenon. Isaac and Jessica looked to Adhira for reassurance that Stephen was unaffected.

"All our monitors are working without issue and Stephen's vital signs are stable, no significant changes," said Adhira.

Jessica asked over the radio link, "What can you tell us?"

"I can almost see through to the other side in places," Stephen responded. "The energy seems to shift and move slightly, like the movement of water."

"How do you feel?" Isaac asked.

"I was a little nervous as I approached, but I'm fine now. I can't feel that anything has changed," Stephen replied.

After a short time, Stephen came back so they could access the results of all the monitors. Adhira did a thorough medical check and was happy to report that he was well. There were no noticeable effects from his proximity to the energy field.

The team had a discussion and agreed that they would wait twenty-four hours before moving on to the next step, which would be for Stephen to come into physical contact with the phenomenon. Until then they would continue to monitor Stephen's health and get some food and sleep.

The next day, the team awoke refreshed and somewhat eager to move forward. Adhira again checked that Stephen was healthy and had suffered no ill effects, before equipping him with the vital signs monitors for the next test.

Out at the site of the energy field, Stephen approached and stopped just in front of the wall. "Are we all good to go?" he asked over the radio.

His colleagues did a final check on everything before Isaac replied, "All looking good."

Stephen then raised his left arm and placed his hand into the field. Adhira monitored him closely, while Thomas stood with his pistol at his side, ready to protect Stephen or stop whatever may come through from the other side.

"It's a slightly odd feeling, like my hand is immersed in an area filled with static energy or something, but otherwise I feel fine," said Stephen.

"That should be enough," Isaac replied.

Stephen withdrew his hand and lowered his arm to his side, and then he turned and walked back to the team and their small mobile research camp. Again, Adhira did all the checks that she could think of, with a focus on his hand, but found nothing out of the ordinary.

After they all heard the results, they knew the next step was for Stephen to walk through to the other side while wearing a tether. Worst-case scenario, they would use the tether to pull him back. In preparation, they once again checked the area with a camera, looking for clues as to the time period he would be entering. The footage continued to show a countryside landscape with no people in sight. Still, wary of threats, Thomas gave Stephen a pistol for self-protection.

Stephen approached the wall as he had the previous two times, and then he stepped forward and into the blue energy. It wasn't a doorway in the way he had expected; it took a few steps to reach the edge of the energy field and he felt a little resistance as he moved.

Once he emerged on the other side, the first thing Stephen noticed was the air quality – it felt much cleaner and fresher as he breathed it in. All those decades of burning fossil fuels had made the air of the present quite poor in quality. He tried the radio, but as expected he got no response from the team. Then he looked at his watch and found it was still working, which was a positive.

Looking up to check out his surroundings, Stephen saw exactly what the camera footage had shown, a countryside location with no habitation visible in the immediate area. This was intended to be a short test, lasting between five and ten minutes at the most, and so Stephen turned and walked back through the energy field. Again it pushed against him as he walked, but it felt like no more than a strong wind.

The team gathered to listen to Stephen's report. He described the scene on the other side, the quality of the air there and the resistance he felt as he walked through the energy field. Adhira reviewed the data from the health monitors and gave Stephen a check-up, but there was little need: he continued to be as healthy as before.

It would be extremely difficult to establish the time period beyond the energy field and further useful information simply by surveying the area around the doorway. To get more answers, they would need to go on an expedition. But first they needed to make preparations.

Jessica and Isaac returned to the research facility to provide an update on the situation and to make a few arrangements. The facility had a number of security personnel, and they needed some of them to stand guard around the energy walls. Plus, they wanted research teams to monitor and study the energy while Isaac, Jessica and their team explored the other side of one of these doorways.

The current hypothesis was that they would be going either to a pre-industrial time or to a point far in the future where nature had fixed the damage humanity had done to the planet. They wanted one more team member, someone who had a good knowledge of history. If they were going to be travelling to the past, it would be ideal to have someone along who could offer information about the time period. Unfortunately, in a facility mostly consisting of experimental scientists, there wasn't anyone with a solid knowledge of history. These were people who focused on the future and its possibilities, not what had come before. So they had to move forward without a historian.

Chapter 5: The Other Side of the Doorway

With people in place to monitor and study and to protect against any potential aggressors, the little group of six was ready to make the expedition to the other side of the doorway through time. At this point they had no clue whether this would be a trip to the past or the future, and this was concerning. If the trip took them back in time, they ran the risk of altering the past, which meant their present may also be altered. On the positive side, they hadn't seen anyone in the area where they would emerge, and they could ensure anything like a pistol was well concealed before they ventured outwards from their arrival point. Larger items that they couldn't conceal would remain near the doorway.

They each stepped though, one by one, carrying equipment between them. Adhira, Thomas and Jessica would stay near the doorway. They didn't know at this point whether the temporal doorway was stable, so it was essential that some of the team stay behind. If there were any changes, they could radio the others. Although they couldn't radio through the temporal field, short-wave radios worked fine within the same time period. Jessica would monitor the energy field, Adhira would set up in case they had a medical emergency, and Thomas would protect them both and give the others a secure position to return to.

This left Isaac, Stephen and Laura free to explore. Laura carried a first-aid kit and an HK USP pistol for protection. They knew the nearest town would be a few miles away towards the east. Towns often changed with the times, but had existed in some form for hundreds or thousands of years. London, for example, was estimated to have existed for two thousand years, but had changed greatly over time.

As they travelled, they noticed an absence of power lines and transmission towers. They saw no modern roads, no tarmac or concrete, but they did see well-trodden paths, which suggested that people ventured into the area, but only on foot. Much of this was seen at a distance using binoculars that Isaac carried, so these were only superficial observations.

They came across a few trees with ripe apples hanging from the branches. Isaac reached up and grabbed one of the apples and took a bite. It had a good, strong flavour. The apples on the tree was a positive sign: healthy trees and fruit suggested a supportive environment. Stephen and Laura picked apples too, and they ate as they continued their walk towards the nearest town.

They arrived at a small wood. In the present, this wood lay in between two towns but was intersected by a road. Either the road hadn't been built yet or a lack of maintenance meant it was no longer there. As they moved closer, they found a well-trodden path in place of the road. The path wasn't used by people alone – they could see horseshoe impressions among the shoe prints on the track.

Isaac and Laura thought it best to stay off the road. They could travel alongside the road but in the forest brush, where they could hide in the undergrowth if needed. They moved more slowly through the brush, but once they neared the edge of the wood, they saw that they had been wise to move covertly. In the distance they could see men on horseback and their clothing was from medieval times.

Granted, people had carried out historical re-enactments up to the modern era, so this wasn't conclusive, but it was looking increasingly likely that they were in the past.

Isaac, Stephen and Laura kept low and under the cover of the foliage as they waited for the men on horseback to do whatever they were here to do – which appeared to be hunting, as they left with two rabbits. Once the men were out of sight and wouldn't hear them, the team of three continued their journey.

When they were close enough, Isaac looked through the binoculars to see the town. Now he was sure they were in the past, as he was looking at a town from centuries before his time. Isaac passed the binoculars to Stephen and Laura so that they could see for themselves. This was a time ruled by the Church and the crown, and opposing either would mean death. If you weren't a nobleman, priest or knight, then this was a dangerous time to be in.

Stephen radioed back to the others to warn them of when they were and that caution was needed. The three of them needed to get back to the temporal doorway without being seen or heard or doing anything that could alter the timeline. It took time and patience, but they managed to get back without being detected. They carefully collected all their equipment, making sure that they would leave no evidence of their visit behind, and then stepped back through to their own time.

Now they knew that they had opened a door to another time. But this wasn't the only doorway; they knew of another one not too far away.

Jessica said, "We need to confirm how many of these doorways exist and if they all go to the same time."

Isaac replied, "I agree. We should start with the next closest door and see whether it goes to the same time period. Then we could use the helicopter at the research facility to explore how many of these doorways through time we've created."

Chapter 6: The Other Doorways

As Isaac finished his sentence, he heard a voice from behind. It was Michael, one of the local residents, and he was asking when they would get answers.

Isaac explained, "We're part of a research team and we've been working on a project called Salvation which was created to establish whether we could open a doorway through time. Our experiment hasn't worked out as we'd expected. The blue energy wall here is some type of doorway in time, and we've learned that it leads back to the Middle Ages. We believe more doorways like this exist. Let me be clear: we have yet to establish how many exist and where they go to, or should I say *when* they go to. And we have no idea whether they are stable. All I can tell you is what we've discovered so far. We must continue our research and fix our mistake before any unforeseen consequences can occur."

Michael stood quietly for a moment, like he was processing what had just been shared with him. After his short pause, he asked, "What should we do?"

Isaac said, "Allow my team and I to continue our work while you continue with your normal life as best you can. I'll share anything else we learn with you."

"Thank you for being honest with me. I'll tell the others and we'll leave you to your work."

Jessica waited until Michael had left before asking, "Why did you tell him so much?"

"If we'd hidden the truth from the residents then they could have started taking action on their own, with unknown results," said Isaac. "Or they could have turned against us, and we may need their help at some point, so it's best to include them and keep on the best of terms with them."

With the residents accepting the situation, at least for the time being, the small research team relocated their equipment and camp to the next closest temporal rift. They made no assumptions that this one would be the same as the first, and followed the same step-by-step investigation to ensure that this rift was also a doorway and safe.

The early tests showed that people were gathered on the other side. The people at the front were police officers. They wore pointed helmets and were smartly dressed, and they weren't carrying the equipment of modern-day officers. Beyond them, behind a police barrier, were civilians. Their clothing, coupled with the look of the police officers, gave the team the impression that the period was around the 1980s.

Jessica spoke first. "This is going to be very different from before. The people on the other side already know about the temporal rift and they won't fear the unknown in the way someone from the Middle Ages would."

Stephen added, "People from the more recent times should be more considered and thoughtful in their actions, which is a positive for us. They should be willing to listen and less likely to make unwise decisions. From my perspective, the worst case would be someone like Genghis Khan and his army being on the other side, waiting to come through to conquer."

"Knowing the circumstances, what do we do next?" asked Jessica.

"I believe we should act the same as we did with the locals from our own time," said Isaac. "We should be honest and share the facts as we know them."

"I agree," said Stephen. "That's fine for this situation, but we'll have to assess each case individually."

Laura said, "You're scientists, so you seek to understand the unknown. But others may fear it, and this could lead to difficult times ahead."

Adhira added, "So far we've been fortunate. The test hasn't caused any side effects from temporal energy, no significant changes in aging. But history is full of conflict and war, and if we've opened a door to any of those times then we could have made the present worse than the future we were trying to avoid."

"Everyone here has a good point and we should all consider them as we progress," said Isaac. "But we need to establish the full effects of the recent test and deal with the fallout. For now, I'm going to step through and speak to those on the other side of this temporal doorway. Would anyone like to join me?"

"Nobody should be time-travelling alone; I'll come with you," said Laura.

"Thank you, Laura. If you all agree, I think the best thing you can do while we're away is to find any other temporal rifts," said Isaac.

A resounding "Agreed" came from the others.

Isaac and Laura grabbed whatever they thought would be useful and then stepped through the blue energy. Surprised faces greeted them. The police advanced on them and instructed them to drop to their knees with their hands in the air. Laura instinctively moved her hand towards her pistol, ready to defend herself and Isaac. The police were acting on instinct and following their training. They didn't know who these people were, or their intentions. All they knew was that they had come from something nobody yet understood, so they would feel more comfortable with the strangers in handcuffs. As the police came closer, Laura raised her pistol to keep them at a distance. Then Isaac stepped between the police and Laura to try to de-escalate the situation.

"We're friendly. Laura, lower your weapon; we're starting off on the wrong foot," he said.

The tension eased as Isaac spoke; hearing words spoken in English with a native accent must have alleviated the fear of the police officers. Laura lowered her weapon but kept it in her hand.

One of the police officers said, "Who are you? What do you want?"

"We only want to talk, to share information with you about the mystery behind us," replied Isaac.

Most people gathered at the energy field wanted answers to their questions, so they were willing to start a dialogue. Isaac began by sharing the same information that he had shared with the residents of the village in his time. The people of the past had more questions and Isaac answered those that he could. After talking, the people were more relaxed and open. Although technology had changed since the 1980s, people hadn't much, and so Isaac and Laura were able to get along with them fairly well.

During a quiet moment when nobody would overhear her, Laura asked Isaac, "Don't you think that you took a big risk coming here?"

Isaac said, "Not really. If they hadn't responded as I hoped then I would have quickly grabbed you and jumped back through the temporal rift. It's unlikely they would have followed us through if they were that fearful."

While Isaac and Laura were building a relationship with the people of the 1980s, Jessica and Thomas set out in search of other temporal rifts. Stephen and Adhira wanted to stay behind in case Isaac and Laura needed help, and they would continue working in the meantime.

After some time on the road, Jessica and Thomas came to another wall of temporal energy. This now meant that there were temporal anomalies on three sides. They travelled along the edges of these rifts to discover that they intersected with each other; there were no gaps between these phenomena. They couldn't check the fourth direction, as they reached the ocean before they encountered any temporal energy barrier.

Thomas had learned how to pilot a helicopter in his time with the army, so he and Jessica returned to the research facility to get the aircraft. Thomas did the usual safety checks before they took off, eager to establish whether another doorway in time existed out in the ocean in the fourth direction. It took some time, but eventually they found another wall of blue energy in the Irish Sea.

So far as Thomas and Jessica could see, they were surrounded by doorways to other times with no gaps between them. Which meant they were cut off from the world of their own time.

Chapter 7: The Future

With the group reunited, they each shared what they had learned. There were at least two more time periods to explore. They decided that Jessica and Thomas would return to the research facility and use the helicopter to travel through the ocean barrier. Once through, they would head for Ireland, so they could establish which time period they were visiting. Meanwhile, Isaac, Adhira and Laura would head for the doorway to the south, while Stephen stayed behind. They figured at least one person should remain in the present to monitor the energy fields and be available if needed.

When Isaac, Adhira and Laura reached their destination, they continued with the scientific approach they had used with the first two temporal rifts. The camera footage showed a thriving countryside ecosystem, but they saw no animals or people. The tests showed the environment to be safe, so they gathered their equipment and stepped through.

The air was fresh, as it had been in the Middle Ages, but this didn't mean they were in the same time period. Adhira set up to test the soil and environment to see whether she could establish the time period. Isaac and Laura started walking, heading for where a small village existed in the present, a few miles to the south.

When they arrived at the location, they saw no village, just greenery. There were two possibilities: either the village had yet to be built or they were so far into the future that there were no visible signs that anything was once there. Although time could hide the past, it was still there if you dug down far enough – this was how the dinosaurs were discovered. Laura radioed back to Adhira to provide an update and to advise that Isaac was attempting to locate any buried evidence of civilisation.

While Isaac and Adhira were attempting to identify which time period they were in, Thomas and Jessica had passed through into a new time themselves and were approaching land. Thomas tried the radio multiple times in order to contact any kind of air control, but there was no response. Jessica asked him to fly over the land so she could view the ground below. Her first observation was the water levels – they were high, so high in places that some areas and towns were submerged. This was the first sign that this could be a future where the ice caps had melted and much of the land had been lost to the rising waters.

Even with rising sea levels, not all the land would be lost, and on the land that remained Jessica could see buildings. Many had fallen down, presumably due to a lack of maintenance. This area must have been without modern society for quite some time.

Jessica asked Thomas to land the helicopter in a clearing near to one of the former developed areas. They left the helicopter to explore the area and see if there were any survivors of this climate change disaster, but they found nobody.

Then, as they were heading back to the helicopter, they were astounded to see a craft in the sky descending towards them. The craft looked a little like a space shuttle, but not one either of them had seen or heard of before. The pair kept back as the craft landed vertically a short distance in front of them. Neither of them had any idea what to expect. Thomas was on alert, as any soldier confronted by the unknown would be. Jessica was more curious than concerned.

The door of the craft opened to reveal a man standing there.

"We know why you're here and, more importantly, that this isn't your time. Come with me. We have much to tell you and we must be quick before the damage is irreversible," said the man.

Jessica began walking towards the craft and gestured for Thomas to follow. He paused for long enough to show his apprehension, but he wasn't going to let Jessica face the unknown alone.

They climbed aboard the craft and Jessica asked, "So, who are you?"

"I'm just the pilot," replied the man. "I was instructed to give you that message and bring you up to the station."

The man then went to the cockpit and took his seat. Jessica and Thomas took seats in the passenger area and strapped themselves in. The craft rose from the ground and then began moving forward, and once it had built up some speed, it turned towards the stars and continued to accelerate upwards. The view from the windows beside Jessica and

Thomas showed blue sky which faded to black as they exited the atmosphere and entered space above Earth.

It took hours to arrive at the orbital space station, which was far larger than anything of their own time. Once they landed, they were met by an escort, who took them through various parts of the station to a meeting room. Along the way, they saw gardens in which vegetables were growing, laboratories, research areas and living quarters. The station appeared to be a self-sufficient colony. Maybe this was another project to ensure humanity's survival.

A woman entered the room. "My name is Alana," she said. "Apologies for being abrupt, but time is limited. You have come from the past through a tear in the space-time continuum which you created with a failed attempt at time travel."

"A tear?" Jessica said, a little puzzled.

"Yes. These aren't doorways through time as you believe – you have shattered the space-time continuum. These tears do allow you to travel from your time to another one, but each time you do so, you're causing more damage."

"How are we causing damage?" asked Thomas.

"I'll explain in simple terms, as you aren't a scientist. When the research team attempted to open a doorway through time, they actually cracked the space-time continuum. Think of it like ice over a pond. That sheet of ice is the space-time continuum. The test was like hitting it with a hammer or pickaxe. The ice is thick, so it didn't break, but you created a hole at the centre and various cracks branched out from the hole. These cracks are what you think of as doorways in time. Each time you go through one of these temporal rifts, you're applying more weight and pressure to the damaged ice. The added pressure causes the crack to expand, weakening the ice sheet even further. Eventually, if the rifts continue to be used, the ice sheet will break apart."

"Surely our small group couldn't have caused much damage by going through once and returning," said Jessica.

"At this point the damage can be reversed," said Alana. "But the more time that passes, the greater the risk. It's not just you who can move through time using these temporal rifts – both sides can cross through to the other. Time periods could bleed into one another. Worse still, if someone from a future time kills someone from the past, they'll create a paradox, and each one of these will do yet more damage, until the whole space-time continuum disintegrates."

"What can we do? We still don't fully understand the results of the test, let alone know how to repair the damage from it," said Jessica.

"Fortunately, we know how to repair the damage," said Alana. "We're from your future, and we have better resources and technology available to help us understand and fix the problem."

"If you have the ability to fix the damage, why are you talking to us?" asked Thomas

"To repair the damage, each tear must be repaired at the same time," Alana said. "But beware: this could leave you trapped in whatever time period you're in at that moment. It would be very dangerous for us to be stuck in the past with our technology; that could have unpredictable results. Also, because we're from a different time to when the fracture occurred, it would cause much more damage if we went between time periods. The fractures centre around you and your time, so you cause the least damage each time you cross a temporal rift. This also explains why the time periods are all within around two thousand years of your time – it's because your time is the focal point."

"This puts us in a quandary," said Jessica. "We're the best chance of repair, but we don't have the knowledge or technology to do it."

"That's why we've been waiting for you to come to us. We can provide all you need to make the repairs," replied Alana.

"What now then?" asked Thomas.

"We've built a craft that will facilitate your travels between time periods," said Alana. "It won't be detectable by any means available to the periods that you visit. We've placed all the necessary equipment aboard the craft. The controls have been designed so that Thomas will be able to pilot it. As I said before, your time and space is the focal point, so the further you travel from the research facility, the fewer temporal rifts you'll encounter. You'll find all the necessary information on a computer on the craft, including what to do if you're successful."

While Jessica and Thomas were learning the truth of the situation, Isaac was jumping to the wrong conclusion. He and Adhira had found evidence of a human civilisation from long ago that indicated they had travelled around one thousand years into the future. This was actually around the time to which Project Salvation had been attempting to open a doorway, so Isaac thought the last test hadn't been unsuccessful after all. It appeared that they had created the very doorway in time that they wanted. They had simply created more doorways than intended leading to additional times.

Chapter 8: Discovering What Lies Ahead

Soon the team had all returned to the present and assembled to discuss their findings. Isaac was keen to offer some good news and explained that one of the temporal doorways led to exactly when they had intended.

Jessica lowered her head for a moment before replying. She didn't want to be the bearer of bad news, but knew it was unavoidable.

"The time period that we visited was sometime in the future. Water levels had risen, and the Earth wasn't able to sustain the population. We were met by people of that future time, and they told us the reality of the situation we are in now."

Jessica then shared all the information that Alana had given them during their brief visit to the orbital space station. She paused for a moment to allow it all to sink in. Around the table, the members of the team were deep in thought, considering their situation and how they would resolve it.

After a few minutes, Isaac spoke. "I think we should begin by reviewing the information on the computer on the craft. We must see what it can tell us about where and when we should go and how we can repair the damage. And we should heed any warnings that it may contain, so we can ensure that we don't make anything worse than it already is."

The team entered the craft and gathered around the computer. "Where do we start?" asked Stephen.

The machine came to life and displayed a world map with various lines, which they deduced were the temporal rifts.

"These are the current temporal regions. Please select a region to display information about the time period within that temporal field," said the computer in a female voice.

Jessica and Thomas recognised the voice; it was Alana's. She must have been one of the people who'd programed the computer with everything they might need to know.

Isaac said, "It's like a ripple effect: the circles grow bigger as they work their way outwards. So the further we travel away from the epicentre, the larger the temporal fields and the fewer there are."

"Some of the lines are favourable," said Stephen. "The one in Russia, for example, which has never been the most densely populated place. It should be much easier there to set up equipment and make repairs without being discovered."

"That's true, but then we also have lines in places in Europe that have been populated and developed for much of the potential time periods," said Jessica.

"The difficultly will very much depend on which time period is in that region," Isaac pointed out. "Look at America. That could be the time of the American Civil War or before Christopher Columbus ever discovered it."

"There may also be times and places that would be hostile to us," said Laura. "Consider Australia before the British sent people there. It would be a land of Aboriginal tribes and they wouldn't welcome outsiders, which we would appear to be. And what about times when women were considered a lower class? It could hard for me, Jessica or Adhira to help in those times."

"You're talking about each rift individually, but didn't our friends from the future say that they all need to be repaired simultaneously?" asked Stephen.

"That's correct," Jessica replied.

"We have a number of problems to address," said Isaac. "We must devise a plan for each time period. The best way for us to do this is to examine the information we have on each time period. Once we know where and when we are going in order to repair each one, we must work out how we can achieve this in the same moment."

"Let's start at the beginning," suggested Jessica. "We have already visited four different time periods and we know what lies in those areas."

"The area to the south should be straightforward and simple," said Laura. "We saw no signs of any inhabitants, so settling there to repair the damage is unlikely to cause us any difficulty."

Thomas asked, "Can we check the information on the computer to confirm?"

Adhira selected the area on the map and said, "Can the computer tell us about this area and its population?"

The computer responded, "This area is part of the thirty-first century. No human population is present in this region."

"The computer responds to voice commands," said Thomas, surprised.

"Yes, I was designed with an interactive program interface," replied the computer.

"That should make things easier," said Adhira.

"Then we have the area to the north, where we have already introduced ourselves and established a friendly relationship. That should be fine too," said Laura.

"The east should be okay as well. We saw nobody around when we travelled to that future," said Thomas.

"We should check our facts about that time period," Isaac said. "You didn't explore much due to the shuttle quickly meeting you and taking you to the orbital station."

Isaac selected the closest area to the east and asked the computer, "Can you tell us if we may encounter anyone here?"

"In this time and area, there are few people due to climate change limiting food availability. The survivors have adapted by returning to a simpler tribal society without technology," explained the computer.

"We already know the western direction could be perilous, given that it is the Middle Ages," said Laura.

"Those are the time periods that border our own, but what do we know about those beyond it?" asked Jessica.

The computer said, "Here is an overview of some of the places and times that you must visit. In Europe, you will be travelling to a time when the Nazi regime is at the height of its power. Next you will enter an area in which the Roman Empire is in full control, and then the time of the British Empire. Afterwards is the period of Genghis Khan. We also have Australia before Britain began sending convicts to the island. There is an area in Russia, but not at a time of any empire or conflict. In America, the time is pre-colonisation, so the land has various Native American tribes. You will also need to travel to Latin America, into remote parts of Brazil, where the Amazon rainforest is thick and full of life. You must travel to a few other regions too, but these are areas with few people and little chance of being discovered."

"So, we now know to where and when we will be travelling, but how do we repair the rifts when we get there?" asked Isaac.

The computer responded, "In the cargo area you will find a number of temporal stabilisation emitters. These must be set up close to the temporal rifts, and once activated they will begin repairing the damage to the space-time continuum."

Stephen said, "But how can we activate all of them at the same time without being trapped in a time that isn't our own?"

Jessica replied, "Using a timer would seem to be the most logical option. We set an identical countdown clock on each temporal stabilisation emitter. Then they can all activate simultaneously, allowing the repairs to be completed while also giving us the chance to reach our own time before the counters hit zero."

"Computer, is this approach possible?" asked Isaac.

"Yes, a timer feature was included in the design of the temporal stabilisation emitters," replied the machine.

"The next question is, how long do we set the timers for?" asked Jessica. "How long will it take us to travel to each place and time and set up the emitters safely without their being damaged or discovered?"

"Couldn't we do a trail run in a safe time and place, like the one to the south, to help answer some of those questions?" asked Adhira.

"That's a good idea," said Isaac "So far we don't know how heavy these units are or how long it will take to set one up. So I think we'll do a test run like Adhira suggests, and then we can plan our next steps."

Chapter 9: The Trial Run

Michael and several other residents came to see Isaac, as they had been told nothing more about the situation and how the team's investigations were progressing.

"We've been patient and left you to your work. However, you've told us nothing since I last asked you for answers. Many of us are concerned, and you aren't helping by staying silent," said Michael.

"I apologise, but events have occurred very quickly, and we find ourselves working against the clock to avoid catastrophe," Isaac replied.

"I don't know how long you have on your clock, but we have problems developing here and now," said Michael. "Although we have local sources of water and power, food is another matter. The homes and shops have been checked and within weeks we'll have nothing left, and there are no farms to produce more."

"We don't know how long we have to repair the damage, but if we can't fix the space-time continuum then it will collapse, and that will be the end of everything," Isaac explained.

Michael asked, "So what do we do, escape to another time?"

"Nobody can go to the past. The more people use the doorways, the more damage is done and the less time we have left," Isaac told him.

He considered telling Michael and the residents more, but he thought it best to keep things simple and direct. Plus, the more time he spent sharing information, the more he was delaying the efforts to do what must be done.

As the residents huddled together, discussing the situation amongst themselves, Isaac decided to extricate himself so that he could return to the others and continue with the next step of their plan.

"I'm sorry, but I must leave. We have a way to correct our past mistake and it requires my time and attention. Please continue as you have, and do not attempt to cross over to another time. With luck, I will have good news for you soon," said Isaac, and he left.

Once aboard the craft with the necessary supplies and equipment, Isaac indicated to Thomas that it was time to go. The craft, which they had affectionately named *Hope*, took to the sky and headed south to the future time period.

Stephen asked, "So once we arrive, which one of us is going to grab the emitter and head through to get it set up?"

"Shouldn't we all go through?" said Jessica. "That way each of us can see how to set up an emitter. After all, it's more than likely that we won't be doing every time period as a group."

Isaac said, "Jessica's right. Splitting up either individually or in small teams will mean that we can save time. Also, as Laura mentioned, it could be very hard for some of us to be in certain times and places, so we should all go and learn about setting up the emitters."

Hope was a fast craft; it needed to be in order to cover ground in the quickest time possible. They soon arrived and landed close to the temporal rift. They all went to the cargo bay, not knowing what these emitters would look like or how big and heavy they were. Clearly, Alana and the others from the future had considered many possibilities. The emitters were in pieces that could fit into a good-sized rucksack. They grabbed one of the units and placed the chassis, power core and other components in one of the rucksacks.

Laura had done a quick count of the units while the others were carefully packing the test unit and she said, "I think we have more units than time zones."

Jessica replied, "I'm not surprised. They seem to have planned for different scenarios, so it makes sense that they've provided spares."

It took less than an hour to set up the temporal stabilisation emitter.

Thomas said, "In this time we can leave it like this, in the open, but in other times we're going to need to hide or camouflage the device."

They all knew Thomas had a good point and nodded in agreement. Nobody could know how a knight of the medieval period or a Roman soldier, for example, would react to a device. It would need to be hidden or its placement carefully chosen.

Isaac said, "We now know how long it will take to set up a device when we have no people to worry about, but we'll need to allow time for finding the right placement or hiding it in other times. Now we need to decide how long we need in order to place these in every time period and get back to the present."

"I think we should be conservative with our estimations," said Jessica. "We have no idea what obstacles we'll encounter in each time."

"And we don't have a plan for who's going where," added Stephen.

"I have a few thoughts on those best suited for certain times," said Isaac. "Laura is already known in the '80s period, so I believe it would be logical for her to take care of that one. The Middle Age rift is nowhere near any settlement, so given the low risk of encountering locals, I think that Jessica might be comfortable with that one. Anybody else have any thoughts?"

Stephen said, "I could take care of the future time to the west."

"This time period is mostly done, but I could stay to set the timer and then head back to the research facility while you're taking care of the other time periods," said Adhira.

"I think that we should try to stick to the places and times where we'll fit in best," Jessica said.

Thomas added, "We also need to consider flight time for travelling to and from each of these destinations."

"I don't think we can plan in too great detail," said Jessica, "because we can't consider every eventuality – we don't have the time or knowledge to do so. I think we should set a time window now, and then proceed as we've discussed so far. Then we can consider what's next afterwards."

"Does anyone disagree?" asked Isaac.

A resounding "No" came from the group.

After some discussion, the group agreed that two weeks should be long enough to place each emitter and return, allowing time for any setbacks. Adhira stayed behind to set the timer on the already placed emitter, which *Hope*'s computer would match on all the other emitters before losing communications as they exited the current time period.

Chapter 10: The Unexpected

Thomas headed for the next closest temporal rift, where Jessica would disembark with everything she needed to set up the emitter for the repair of that rift. As soon as Jessica was clear and signalled to Thomas to go, he headed towards the north, so Laura could do the same in the next area. Then it was time for the final drop-off, of Stephen in the future period. Isaac would remain on *Hope* so that he could do some more research and maybe plan for the next areas.

As the temporal rift was just off the coast of Ireland, Stephen would need to set up the emitter as close as possible. Unfortunately, this meant some walking, as the immediate area wasn't suitable for a landing. As Thomas landed *Hope*, Stephen grabbed everything he needed. It would only take an hour or so to reach the ideal position and then at least another hour to get set up. Given that Thomas and Jessica hadn't encountered anyone on their previous visit, they thought it should be safe for Thomas to set up alone.

It seemed odd that the helicopter wasn't where it had been left, but given that they expected to be in this time and place for less than three hours, it didn't seem worth investigating. Stephen grabbed the rucksack with the emitter and headed towards the coast. Thomas and Isaac knew that he should be back shortly, so they remained with *Hope*. Based on the information they had so far, all four time zones should be uneventful and quick to complete, so research on the next areas seemed the best use of Isaac's time.

When three hours had passed and Stephen hadn't returned or made contact, Isaac and Thomas grew concerned. They knew that in this time period there was a small population in Ireland, but they hadn't seen anyone the last time they visited, which was for a longer time, so they'd thought it unlikely they would encounter anyone this time.

Isaac said, "Too much time has passed. Something's gone wrong."

"Agreed. I'll go and investigate what's happen to Stephen," Thomas replied.

"Wouldn't it be best if I went? You're the only person who can pilot *Hope*."

"I can track Stephen and I have combat training; I think my skills are more suited to dealing the various possibilities than your own."

Isaac nodded. "Unfortunately, I have to agree with you."

Thomas asked, "Have you ever fired a gun before?"

"Yes, I learned with the army cadets when I was young."

"Good, take this and defend yourself if necessary," said Thomas as he handed Isaac an assault rifle.

"Be cautious," Isaac called as Thomas left.

Thomas headed in the direction Stephen had gone and tracked his course through footprints, broken branches and trodden ground. Eventually, he reached the coast where Stephen must have been setting up the emitter, but now the emitter and Stephen were gone.

Thomas examined the area and found a spot where it looked like Stephen had fallen. Tracks suggested that someone had come up behind him and knocked him out. Thomas could see other tracks with deep footprints, the heavier pattern suggesting that the person was carrying extra weight, probably Stephen and the equipment.

Thomas radioed Isaac: "Looks like Stephen and the equipment have been taken by the natives. Be on your guard. I'm going to follow the tracks and see if I can rescue Stephen."

After around thirty minutes, Thomas came to the entrance to a cave. He saw a group of men, one of them carrying Stephen over his shoulder. The men on the ground were the opposite of the people he'd met in the orbital space station. Their clothes were old and torn in places, and their footwear was no better. As they moved into the cave, Thomas followed as stealthily as possible; he didn't want these people to see or hear him.

The cave was lit by burning torches – to Thomas it looked like the survivors on Earth had regressed a couple of thousand years. The men were moving deeper into the large cave, and Thomas headed for a ledge above from where he could watch what occurred below. The ceiling was black with soot, probably from the burning torches or campfires used for light and warmth.

The men brought Stephen to three others, probably those in a position of authority. They struck Stephen across the face, attempting to wake him up from his unconscious state. He began to wake, groggy, then reached for his head, likely where he had been struck earlier.

The man in the centre of the three – the leader, Thomas assumed – spoke: "You have been found with the ancient evil. Do you have anything to say in your defence?"

Still disorientated, Stephen replied, "What ancient evil?"

"The ancient evil that made the world what it is now," said the leader.

Stephen, who was still coming to his senses, said, "I don't know what you're talking about."

One of the people who'd brought Stephen to the cave then threw parts of the emitter onto the ground at his feet. "This ancient evil!"

After another moment Stephen was more lucid and he said, "It's a harmless piece of technology, designed to repair the rift."

This caused anger in the leader. "No, technology isn't harmless. It's the ancient evil that destroyed the world and raised the oceans, making our survival such a struggle now. We will not allow you to bring down more destruction upon us with this evil!"

Thomas and Stephen realised now that the survivors blamed technology for all the strife in their lives and the changes the world had undergone. Though technology had played a part, of course the real culprits were humans themselves who controlled the technology.

Thomas was considering his options. He could try to reason with these men, explain the situation and correct their misunderstandings about the past. Or he could be the soldier he was trained to be. These people weren't a significant threat and he could stop them without killing any of them. But he and Stephen still needed to complete their mission here and set up the emitter – which was best for the end goal?

Thomas decided that making enemies here wouldn't help anyone, so he would try to reason with the men. If that failed then he still had his gun in his leg holster.

The leader said, "We have no choice but to sentence you to death. It's the only way to ensure our survival."

Thomas stood up and said, "Wait!"

Everyone looked up at Thomas, including Stephen, who had a look of relief on his face.

"You have things wrong," said Thomas. "Not all technology is evil. You're going to kill an innocent man who's only trying to help you." He pulled the torch from his webbing pouch and switched it on. "Look, this technology is harmless. It's not all evil."

A look of fear appeared on the faces of the men. They must have expected something terrible to happen as soon as technology was used. But as the seconds and minutes passed… nothing. No end of the world, no consequences at all.

The men looked at the leader, who seemed to be judge, jury and maybe even executioner, waiting for his response.

Stephen wanted to add his voice to Thomas's. "If all technology will have such disastrous consequences, why didn't anything happen after I brought my equipment here?"

One of the two men next to the leader said, "And nothing happened after they came in the machine last time."

The leader replied, "Only because we pulled it apart."

"So that's what happened to the helicopter," Thomas said under his breath. "My light is still on, but the world hasn't ended," he said loudly. "Could it be that your information is wrong, that not all technology is evil?"

"We're only here to repair the damage the evil of the past has done. I swear," said Stephen.

The native people couldn't deny that no harm had come from the technology. Plus, survival was hard, and they would welcome things being easier and better for them. These things likely convinced them to change their position.

After some time passed, the leader said, "Okay, do what you must to repair the damage from the ancient evil. But if you're lying then you'll be the first to die."

Stephen said, "I must set up the equipment where you found me. It will be here for two weeks and must be allowed to do its work."

"We will allow this and protect the machine till the world is fixed," said the leader.

Thomas kept his hand near his holster until they left the cave, and then he was able to relax a little more. Thomas radioed to Isaac to provide an update. They would be returning to collect another emitter so they could set up and leave. This time, however, Stephen wasn't going alone to complete the setup – Thomas insisted on going along to watch his back.

Laura's trip to the '80s was less eventful. She was greeted by the same policeman they had spoken to before, and she shared her knowledge, as she knew Isaac would have done the same in her position. The policeman informed her that a few people wanted to come to the future and wouldn't accept the doorway being closed, so he said that he would keep some of the information secret, as this was in everyone's best interests.

Unfortunately, it transpired that Jessica's trip also hadn't gone as planned, because she wasn't at the research facility when the others arrived.

Chapter 11: Search for the Missing Member

The team gathered to discuss how their attempts to set up in the first few time zones had gone. Adhira had not had any problems, and neither had Laura. They were shocked when Stephen recounted his eventful story.

"Going forward, we can't make the same assumption as before: that it should be easy. If we have more surprises like that, we'll never be successful," said Isaac.

The words sank in deeply with the team, particularly as Jessica had failed to return.

After a pause, Thomas asked, "What do we do now?"

"Someone needs to go to the Middle Ages region," said Isaac, "to make sure the emitter is set up and see what happened to Jessica. Meanwhile, the timers are already running, so we need the rest of the team to continue the work of repairing the space-time continuum."

"I could go to the Amazon rainforest," said Stephen. "I used to like going exploring when I was younger, so I'm familiar with that kind of environment. It would be ideal if Adhira could join me. Those parts have lots of dangers – venomous animals, poisonous plants and predators – so a doctor and companion team would improve the odds."

"I won't be able to land in the jungle, so you'll need to make your way from the closest point available," said Thomas.

"While you're setting up in that region, I'll go and set up in the Middles Ages period, if Jessica hasn't already done so. Then I'll see if I can find her or establish what's happened to her," said Isaac.

"Would you like some company?" asked Laura.

"You'd be more than welcome to accompany me," Isaac replied.

The two teams quickly organised themselves and headed for their respective destinations.

As Isaac and Laura passed through the rift, they could see the emitter had been smashed to pieces. Fortunately, the power core hadn't been compromised, as the release of the energy in the wrong manner could have been devastating. After a scout around the area, they noticed horse tracks heading towards the town they had seen from a distance on their previous visit.

"We need to set up the spare emitter I brought along, as this one is unusable," said Isaac. "Given the situation, it would be best if it were hidden and camouflaged. You'd be much better suited to this than me with your experience. Would you be able to do that while I follow the horse trail and look for Jessica?"

"Yes, I can do that. But isn't it risky for you to go alone?" replied Laura.

"You'll be able to catch up with me once you're finished here. It's a risk, but it's worth it to save us some time. I'll be proceeding very cautiously, especially after the surprises of that future we just visited."

Isaac gathered the binoculars and a few other useful items and then began walking. He didn't look back at Laura, but focused on the path ahead of him. Laura quickly got to work – the quicker she could set up and hide the emitter, the faster she could head after Isaac and Jessica.

Isaac tried to stay off the path as he moved, walking in the foliage where possible, and he kept checking the path ahead with the binoculars for any dangers. Eventually, he came to the town they had seen on their first visit to the time period. Unlike on that visit, the town wasn't only populated with peasants; there were several knights and horses. The knights were dressed for battle, wearing chainmail or heavy armour, which was odd. Why would there be lots of knights in a town with nothing but peasants and farmers? Even if they were resisting the will of the local lord or the crown, two or three knights would be more than enough to bring them into line.

Isaac needed to go into the town to find answers, but his clothes would attract attention. He needed clothes of the period to disguise himself. He considered two options: sneak into town and try to steal some clothes there, or find someone on the outskirts and borrow their clothes. Isaac spotted a man wearing a cloak approaching the town but still some distance away. This seemed perfect. Isaac could wear the cloak over his clothes and then move freely through the town.

Isaac had a sedative from the medical kit with him, so he could easily render his target unconscious without attracting attention. He slowly approached the man from behind, wrapped his arms around him, injected the sedative into his neck, and then held his hand over his mouth until the sedative took effect and the resistance stopped. Isaac then dragged the man into the long, tall grass and took his cloak.

As Isaac entered the town, he saw that the people appeared to be nervous and anxious. It could have been the presence of the knights, but they didn't seem to be taking any action. It was like they were on their guard, waiting for some enemy or danger to reach the town.

As he walked around the town – speaking to no one, because he wouldn't be competent at speaking old English – nobody took much interest in him. All seemed quiet. He noticed a poster on the wall and one word stood out: "Witch". Now the presence of the knights and the people's demeanour made more sense: they were fearful of a witch.

Isaac left the town so he could radio Laura. "The local town is crawling with knights and has posters relating to a witch. I'm worried that Jessica was discovered and they jumped to the conclusion that the temporal rift is magic and she's the witch controlling it."

"I can see how someone from this time would jump to that conclusion, but what can we do?" said Laura.

"We can rescue her. I can find out where she's being kept and then we can break her out."

"We'd be seen, and who knows what damage that would do."

"Not if you can hide us with a few smoke grenades; that could be dismissed as fog."

"I do have three with me, but what about the bars of the jail?"

"If you bring me the power source and a few of the components from the damaged emitter, I could build a makeshift cutter."

Laura said, "I'll grab what we need, then meet up with you."

"If you could procure some clothes of this time period on your way, that would help greatly," Isaac added.

They found the jail where Jessica was being held. Fortunately, witches were feared, so the people wanted to stay as far away as possible until the execution. There were knights nearby, but only as close as they needed to be. A smoke grenade concealed Laura and Isaac's entry into the building, and then there were only two men between them and Jessica, one guard and a jailer. A strong punch from Isaac knocked out the jailer, while Laura used a baton to deal with the guard.

"You've come to rescue me," said Jessica, surprised.

"Can't talk. We need to be quick and quiet," Isaac replied as he quickly removed the cutter from his backpack and began melting the lock on the door. Meanwhile, Laura kept an eye out, prepared for any attack.

As soon as Isaac had the door open, he grabbed Jessica and signalled to Laura that they would be leaving now. Much of the smoke from the first grenade had dissipated, so Laura pulled the pin on a second and released it into the town. As soon as the smoke began to fill the air like a thick fog, they started moving quickly.

Some commotion could be heard – probably the townsfolk, and maybe the knights too, concerned about the sudden fog. The three visitors from the future were close to escaping the town, but the smoke was again clearing. Laura used the last smoke grenade to cover their exit from the town, but they still needed to make it back to the rift before they would be safe.

Chapter 12: The Escape

Stephen and Adhira were miles away from their destination, but it had been impossible to land any closer. This was a time before mankind had cut down and thinned out the rainforest, so it was mostly dense jungle. The two moved through the jungle as quickly as they could, but they also needed to take care as they headed for their destination. The jungle was hot and humid; it was tougher for Stephen than Adhira, as he was less suited to the climate.

They both knew that tribes existed in the Amazon that had never had contact with the outside world. This had remained true even in the future timeline, where they had been given all the information they had. Stephen and Adhira couldn't know if they would encounter one of these tribes and if so how they would react to outsiders. Given recent events, Stephen almost expected to meet a tribe and for them to be less than friendly, but it turned out that the opposite was the case. They did encounter a tribe, but despite showing trepidation about the visitors, they were friendly.

Unfortunately, they had no common language, but a few gestures like giving water and food seemed to allow Stephen and Adhira to be welcomed as friends. Adhira had spent time working with Doctors Without Borders and had visited many parts of the world, meeting with people who were less fortunate and offering her aid, and this meant she was accustomed to being with others without a common language. That made this situation much easier. Adhira couldn't help but notice how little it took to be welcomed by this Amazonian tribe. In most places she had visited, it had taken far longer to build a relationship of trust between her and the natives. Maybe no contact with the outside world made them more trusting.

Stephen and Adhira didn't have the luxury of time, so they gave what they could and Adhira cared for a few of the tribe members' injuries and illnesses, and then they continued to the temporal rift to set up the emitter.

Isaac, Jessica and Laura were now outside of the town and able to talk as they walked.

Isaac asked Jessica, "Are you okay? Can you tell us what happened?"

"I'll be fine once we leave this time," she said. "Unfortunately, when I came through the rift this time, I was seen. I knew it was possible that they would go for help, but I thought I could set up and leave before anyone arrived to find me. I was wrong. I saw the knights coming and tried to hide until they passed, but they found the emitter and destroyed it. Then I could see them looking for me. I hadn't thought about them following my tracks, as I'd got into a bit of a panic. They were going to find me, so I sprang out of my hiding place and ran as fast as I could towards the rift. I thought it highly unlikely they would follow me through. But their horses were quick and they caught me before I could jump through. After that I can only remember waking up in the town and being accused of being a witch. I think they were going to execute me."

"Do you need me to take a look at you?" asked Laura.

"I'm fine. I don't think I was hit that hard," Jessica replied.

"We'll get you out of here," said Isaac.

As they were approaching the forest, they looked behind and saw the knights on horseback heading their way.

"If we can make it to the forest and stay low in the foliage then we should be able to stay undetected," said Laura. "It was easy to follow Jessica's tracks, but it'll be much harder in the foliage. The knights would have to climb down from their horses and move the greenery aside – it would take a long time to find us that way."

The three travellers from the future increased their pace to reach the forest and hopefully safety. They made it, just. As the sound of the horse hooves hitting the ground became louder, they dropped to the ground in the undergrowth to make it as hard as possible for them to be found. The knights looked around for any signs of them and listened for any sound, but to no avail. As time passed, it seemed to be a waiting game, until the knights gathered and headed off.

"They've left," said Laura.

"Yes, but their direction suggests they're going to the rift," said Isaac. "They know that's where Jessica was found, and they may have decided to wait for us there."

"I agree, that's the most likely scenario. We'll need to find a way past them," said Jessica.

"We need to do more than find a way around them," said Isaac. "We need them to leave the area and not come back. I'm sure you hid the emitter well, Laura, but I'd imagine with over a week to find it, they would."

"Then we need to find a way to satisfy the knights that their witch problem is gone and won't come back," said Jessica.

"How do we do that?" asked Laura.

"We need to kill Jessica," Isaac replied.

Laura paused as though she couldn't believe what she had just heard.

"You have a flash-bang with you, don't you, Laura?" asked Isaac.

"I have one for an emergency," said Laura.

"We need to collect some combustible material which can be made to look like Jessica from a distance," said Isaac.

"You're going to make it look like I was burned to death," said Jessica.

"Yes, but with a little bit of theatrics to help sell it," Isaac replied.

"Would you like to catch me up with your thinking?" said Laura.

"We'll need to attract the attention of the knights," Isaac explained. "Then, while they aren't too close, I'll confront the witch as a servant of God. They'll just be able to make out that the witch in question is Jessica. Then the flash-bang will blind them, and standing in Jessica's place will be her double, burning until nothing is left. The cutter and power cell can create the fire. Once most of the energy has been discharged, the fire will be hot enough to destroy them too."

It was easy to attract the attention of the knights. Wearing the cloak he had taken earlier, Isaac shouted "Witch!" in a loud voice. Jessica then turned to face him, as the knights began riding quickly towards them. A subtle nod from Jessica when they were close enough let Isaac know to use the flash-bang, while Laura pulled the makeshift rope, made from old roots and greenery, to bring the double up and start the blazing fire. During those few short moments Jessica jumped from her position into a nearby ditch and pulled the cover made from sticks and leaves over her so she wouldn't be seen.

The plan was far from perfect, but it was the best they could come up with given what they had available. Luck was on the side of the travellers from the future, though, as by the time the knights reached Isaac, the fire had left nothing behind but some ash. The knights looked at the mysterious cloaked man who appeared to have destroyed the witch. Isaac kept his head low and well covered by the hooded cloak.

"The will of the Lord is done," he said.

The knights didn't get too close to the mysterious man out of fear, but hearing his words, they made the sign of the cross. Then they lowered their heads and began riding back towards the town.

Isaac then sat on the grass as though he was praying, while Jessica and Laura remained in hiding. They remained like this until the sound of the horses became faint and they were sure that nobody else was around, and then they headed for the temporal rift and back to the safety of their own time.

Chapter 13: Seeking Permission

The group were again united and talked about their latest travels, sharing that they had been successful in setting up emitters in their respective areas. Now they needed to decide where and when to go next. The team looked to Isaac, as he had been doing some research while in that future period.

"Isaac, you've had a chance to review the places and times we still have to visit. What's your input?" asked Jessica.

Isaac said, "One of the destinations ahead of us is one that Stephen, Thomas and I are unlikely to manage. Although the region is peaceful and the people generally friendly, it's the land of the Hopi Native American tribe and they consider the land to be sacred. This tribe has a matriarchal society, where women are clan leaders. So only another woman is likely to be granted access to their land."

"You believe this should be one of our next destinations?" asked Adhira.

"Given the nature of the Hopi people, I believe this would be a good next choice. The question is, who would be best to go?" said Isaac.

"After seeing how well Adhira bonded with the Amazonian tribe, I can't think of anyone better to make contact," said Stephen.

"Thank you. I'd be happy to try to make contact with them and see if they will allow us to visit their land," said Adhira.

"After the bad experiences Stephen and I had, I'll go with you, so you have someone looking out for you," said Jessica.

Adhira thanked her. "It will be nice to have the company."

"I think it should be the same for everyone from this point on: nobody goes alone. We must look out for each other as we travel through these times and places," said Isaac.

Each of the members of the team nodded in agreement. They knew they had been lucky not to lose someone already.

"What other destinations do you have in mind?" asked Thomas.

"Russia should be a safe option," said Isaac. "Very sparsely populated and it's the height of winter with strong snowstorms. It will make landing difficult, so it may be a bit of a journey in very cold conditions. Thoughts?"

"I hate the cold," said Laura.

"We have some very cold times in Canada, so I'm quite accustomed to it. I can join you," offered Thomas.

"Laura and Stephen can do a little research for the next destination and keep the ship secure while we're away then," said Isaac.

Adhira and Jessica disembarked first, and the others continued on *Hope* to their next destination. They had brought a small tablet with all the information that was available on the Hopi, but it wasn't much: unfortunately, so many facts about these people and their culture had been lost to history. Adhira and Jessica set up a small tent not far from the Hopi land so they could read what information was available about the people and their culture. Everything they read suggested the people were friendly, and this had been their downfall. Some of the early visitors from Europe had been less than kind to them and they had come across as pacifists in a time when many nations were expanding their territories.

Fortunately, this was a time before any contact from those nations, so the Hopi would likely still be true to who they were. But Jessica and Adhira would be their first visitors from a strange land. Adhira had similar features and skin tone and could convincingly pass as a member of the Hopi tribe, but Jessica couldn't – her Asian features would stand out. They decided that it would be best to begin with Adhira making contact while Jessica observed from a distance in a place where she could look out for Adhira, although they both felt it was unlikely that Adhira would need backup.

The Hopi were indeed very welcoming. As Adhira approached they were having a meal. She was greeted with words which she believed meant "Hello, friend" and then encouraged to share their meal. Adhira sat down on the ground and ate with the Hopi people. She managed to say thank you; fortunately this phrase was included in the tablet file on the Hopi culture.

Adhira spent the evening observing and where possible joining in with their ceremonies and rituals. She was trying to make the Hopi feel that she was one of them. Towards the end of the evening, Adhira left to join Jessica and share the story of her first interactions with the Hopi.

The next morning, Adhira and Jessica went to forage for food – not for themselves, but so they could offer it as a gift to the Hopi people. It was the only gift that they might accept. They managed to get a small amount of suitable food together.

Later that day, Adhira returned to the Hopi village with Jessica at her side. Jessica was also warmly greeted by the Hopi. Adhira and Jessica gave the food they had gathered that day to the clan mother and then to the others within the village. The Hopi accepted the gift with good spirits. Afterwards, Jessica and Adhira helped in the fields and other areas which were so important to a successful life for the Hopi. They participated in their ceremonies and rituals, and felt that they were being accepted and embraced by the tribe.

While Adhira and Jessica were bonding with the Hopi, Isaac and Thomas were being battered by the cold winds and snow of the Russian winter. There was no reason to have winter weather gear at the Salvation research station, so they'd needed to improvise alternatives, like using sunglasses to protect their eyes. It didn't help that the strong winds meant they couldn't land close to the temporal rift, so they were forced to spend more time in the challenging conditions. This was one occasion for which their friends from the future hadn't covered every possibility; if they had, then they would have provided some gear for this inhospitable place.

Not only did the weather make reaching their destination something of a struggle, but it also caused complications when trying to set up the emitter. The emitter needed to be protected from the elements: they couldn't risk the unit failing before the timer reached zero, and it needed to remain standing, not buried by the falling snow. Isaac found Thomas invaluable: his training and experience in so many different environments from his time with the armed forces meant that they were able to build a shelter for the emitter to protect it from the elements and prevent it from being lost under the snow.

They stayed in the shelter to warm up for a while before beginning the journey back. Isaac looked at the timer while he was regaining the feeling in his extremities. Days had passed since they'd set the first timer for two weeks. Time was running out. They had taken longer in some time periods than expected and they still had the most difficult regions to visit.

Thomas and Isaac were relieved to reach *Hope* after the arduous journey. After taking a little time to warm up, Thomas returned to the cockpit and they began the flight towards Adhira and Jessica.

Once they arrived, they needed to communicate with Adhira and Jessica, but they couldn't risk using the radio in case the women were with the Hopi. They decided that Laura would make her way towards the Hopi village to try to make contact while avoiding the Hopi. Laura was best suited, because if she was seen, the Hopi would be more accepting of a woman than a man.

As she drew closer to the village, Laura saw Adhira and Jessica from a distance using the binoculars. She radioed the others to say that her impression was that Adhira and Jessica had been accepted by the tribe. Laura said that she would wait for either or both to leave, and then they could talk freely about how close they were to being able to enter the Hopi land and set up the stabilisation emitter.

Once it was night-time, Jessica walked out of the Hopi village. Curiously, Adhira didn't follow, but remained in the village with the tribe. Once Jessica was out of sight of the village in the darkness, Laura approached her.

"How are you and Adhira?" she asked.

Jessica turned, somewhat surprised to see Laura, and replied, "We're good. The Hopi have been very welcoming."

"Are you having any success with getting access through their land?"

"Adhira has asked the clan mother and we should have their answer tomorrow."

"Why is Adhira staying while you leave?" Laura asked curiously.

"Adhira has formed a much closer bond with the Hopi," said Jessica, "and she decided to stay whilst they make their decision. I think she is very fond of the people and their ways, and I understand why."

Jessica and Laura returned to the tent, which was not too far away, and then radioed back to the others to give them an update.

The next morning, Laura woke first, and then Jessica shortly thereafter. Jessica had hoped that the clan mother and tribal council would give their approval today and allow them safe passage through their land. Although the Hopi were a very peaceful people, they did have warriors and would use them to defend the sacred land for the good of all the people of the world – at least that was their viewpoint.

That afternoon, Adhira arrived at the tent and shared that the Hopi tribe had agreed to allow them to enter their land. Jessica and Adhira collected their rucksacks. They made their way to the temporal rift, set up the emitter and returned before the day was over.

When they reached *Hope* and shared the story of their time with the Hopi, Adhira appeared a little out of sorts, so Isaac took her aside for a private conversation.

"What wrong?" he asked.

"I've never met people like the Hopi before," she said. "I wish I could stay here with them and protect them from the future that lies ahead of them. I think the world that we come from would've been a better place if they'd flourished instead of being reduced to a tiny group by the events of history."

"I understand," said Isaac. "After what I've read and what you've told us, it would be so easy to be tempted to rewrite history and save the better parts of humanity. But we have no idea what the consequences of such a change would be. We've all been very careful not to change things for the worst, but perhaps at the end of our journey we'll find the hardest part was trying not to change the past for the better."

"I didn't realise you considered such things. You've been leading us with focused determination and listening to us at every step, yet you've also been considering the very things you and the future have warned us against."

"I'm only the leader because someone had to be and nobody else stepped forward. But I'm a dreamer too, which is one of the reasons I pursued science. And I've thought about the opportunity to change the past, staying in the '80s and either steering things in the right direction or leaving a few key instructions to correct our past mistakes. It's extremely tempting to take a little risk, but sometimes we only learn by our mistakes and maybe this has to be one of those times."

"I think you're right. For me the hardest part will be to leave the past as it is."

"I hope you won't mind keeping our little talk between us," said Isaac. "We're running out of time, and the last thing we need is to stop and focus on these thoughts."

"I understand," said Adhira. "It's a conversation for another time."

Chapter 14: Complications

Before moving on to the next destinations, they returned to their own time so they could resupply and gather any items which could be useful in the next time periods. Shortly after landing, Jessica was approached by Michael very discreetly.

Michael spoke quietly: "I'm coming to you because others would question me if I spoke to Isaac directly."

"Won't they question you about approaching me?" replied Jessica.

"Yes, but it's easy to say that I was approaching a beautiful woman for other reasons. That won't raise many questions."

"Thank you for the compliment. Now, what do you need to say so secretly?"

"The others are planning to go to the past," said Michael. "They intend to go in about ten days, once the food supplies run out – then they can say that they had no choice. It's possible that some may try to go sooner, though."

"Isaac has been open and told everyone what's at stake and the dangers of going through the rift. Why would they be so foolish?" said Jessica.

"I'm wise enough to know when something is beyond me, but others may think they know better or that your team are exaggerating the dangers. Then there's the fact that if we go, it could spell doom, but if we stay, we're on borrowed time anyway, so why not take the risk?"

"I appreciate you coming to me and the advance warning. I'll speak to the others," said Jessica, and Michael left.

Once everyone was together, she said, "We have another problem to consider: the residents of the area are planning to go to the past."

Isaac said, "More than one problem, actually. Whilst you were speaking to Michael, another of the residents came to me and handed over a box containing a message from the police officers in the '80s. A small group there intends to come to the future. They want to collect technology and take it back with them to their own time."

"And these issues are on top of the countdown to repair the space-time continuum before it collapses," added Stephen.

"On the positive side," said Jessica, "the residents here are planning to cross over after the timer reaches zero. So as long as nobody jumps the gun, we should be okay on this side. To be safe, though, we should keep coming back after each destination or group of destinations to check on things."

"And the closing of the rifts isn't public knowledge in the '80s," said Isaac, "so they shouldn't feel any urgency to cross into the present. Hopefully, the same will apply to that problem. We will have repaired the space-time continuum before anyone from the '80s attempts to come to the present."

"This was one of the reasons I was concerned about sharing information with the people of different times," said Laura.

"I thought we might need their help at some point and we still may, but I accept it could've been a mistake on my part," Isaac replied.

"What's done is done. We need to decide where and when to go next," said Jessica.

"We have five times and places left to visit, three of which seem high risk and dangerous," said Stephen.

"I'm very worried about the Nazi-controlled area, and the one under the Romans won't be much better," said Isaac. "The safest options remaining are Australia and India, in my opinion."

"The Aboriginal people were only hostile once the colonists tried to take their land and they felt invaded. If we approach them as we did Hopi, then I don't think we'll face too much difficulty there," said Jessica.

"Given how successful you were with the Hopi, do you think you could do the same in Australia?" asked Stephen.

"I think Adhira should get most of the credit for that," said Jessica.

"I could accompany Adhira," Laura offered. "I spent some time in Australia when I was with NATO."

"Thank you," said Adhira, "but I think if someone is going to India, it would be best if I joined them, as that was where I was born and raised. I could probably be more helpful there."

"I won't be as gifted as Adhira in making contact, but I did observe many of her interactions with the Hopi, and with a little research I think Laura and I could be successful in Australia," said Jessica.

"Unless anyone feels better suited, I'll join Adhira in India," said Isaac.

"That makes sense," said Stephen. "India was part of the British Empire at the time, so together you should be able to blend in well. Afterwards, we can focus on the more perilous destinations we must still visit."

Isaac found India to have a warmer climate than was comfortable for him, but after his time in those Russian snowstorms, he wasn't going to complain. Being in this time and place was a welcome change of pace. It was a civilised time when the British and the people of India were on good terms, and his being seen with Adhira was generally accepted, although frowned upon by one or two. This felt more like a tourist trip in comparison with what they had been through before. For Adhira, it was like seeing and living in her own country's history. Never would she have thought when she was sitting in her classroom at school all those years ago that she would one day visit this time period herself.

With Isaac being obviously British, the locals were enthusiastic about accommodating his needs. Isaac and Adhira had no trouble acquiring transport and were free to go where they pleased. They were successful in setting up the emitter and returned to *Hope* in a decent timeframe.

Jessica and Laura, meanwhile, were making contact with the Aboriginal people. These people were different from the Hopi: gifts could be welcomed or seen as an attempt at bribery, so great care had to be taken to offer the right gifts when introducing themselves. They offered a little food and tobacco. Although it might seem unusual, tobacco was a welcome gift, as it was used in Aboriginal ceremonies and sometimes as a medicine.

Jessica followed some of the same steps that she had seen Adhira take with the Hopi. She joined in with their rituals and ceremonies and encouraged Laura to do the same. This helped them to be accepted. Once they had accepted the women, the Aboriginals wanted to reciprocate with gifts, which was an opportunity for Jessica to ask whether they would be allowed to travel across their land briefly. The Aboriginal people gave their approval.

Once the festivities were finished for that day, Jessica and Laura proceeded to the rift. They set up the emitter, before returning to the landing point to join the others.

Chapter 15: The Greatest Danger Lies Ahead

Before considering their next destinations, the team needed to return to their own time and check for local residents trying to reach the past and for any visitors from the past. Although they had security people guarding and patrolling the rifts, it was far too much ground for the small numbers to effectively police. Fortunately, it looked like nobody had travelled from either side of the rift to the '80s. With nothing to keep them in the present, it was time to discuss where and when they should go next.

"I think we've all been avoiding it, but we don't have the luxury any longer: we need to enter the Nazi region. Then we can move east until we've covered the last couple of regions," said Isaac.

"I can't think of a more dangerous place to go," Thomas said.

"I honestly don't know what's best, a smaller group for stealth or strength in numbers," said Isaac.

"It's not much, but I do speak a little German, since I did a few NATO tours there," said Laura.

"I'm sure that will help," Thomas replied.

"Many of us are from countries that were at war with Germany during this period, so the Nazis won't be laying out the welcome mat," said Stephen.

"Who else would be best suited to joining Laura?" asked Isaac.

"I'll be going with whoever goes," said Thomas. "I'm a trained soldier who signed up to serve and protect innocent people. I only left the services because I discovered I was fighting more for money and politics than for people. This time I'll be fighting for the right cause."

"They should have at least one of us scientists with them, so I'll go," said Stephen.

"You're showing a lot of courage," said Jessica.

"To be honest I'm petrified, but you might need me, and I know I can rely on Thomas to save me like he did last time," said Stephen.

"I'll go too," said Isaac. "Somebody needs to stay with *Hope* – it can't fall into Nazi hands. I'm no soldier, but I can shoot a gun if needed."

"I'll stay here," said Jessica. "Someone needs to remain and talk sense to the residents and those from the '80s period if they decide they're going through the rift. Also, with one of us around to keep an eye on things, they might reconsider going through the rift."

"Adhira, it's your choice whether you want to come with us or stay with Jessica," said Isaac.

"Like Stephen, I must reluctantly acknowledge that the chances of you needing a doctor are high, so as much as I'm fearful about going, I'll join you," said Adhira.

"Adhira and Stephen, you aren't alone," said Isaac. "I couldn't be more worried about our next destination. But courage is not the absence of fear, but acting despite fear."

Hope was built so that it wouldn't be detected by radar or other means, and the Nazis wouldn't have anything that would be able to match its speed, but it would be detectable on the ground. Thomas believed the safest place for *Hope* if it couldn't stay on the ground was in the sky. But what if he wasn't there? He realised that he needed to give Isaac some basic lessons in defence just in case.

Laura was also considering the possibilities in this most hostile time and place. She thought that radios wouldn't be enough, and so they should have a tracker in case anyone was separated and needed to be found or rescued. Between Isaac and Stephen, the tracker was a simple problem to solve. They created small beacon devices that could fit into a watch on their wrist.

Isaac had no flying experience, but the controls weren't too complicated for him. It was like driving, just with an up and down added in.

The rift was in the middle of a city, so they landed *Hope* on one of the outer city buildings at night. Then Thomas, Laura and Stephen disembarked. Isaac piloted the craft into the sky, well above the level that any plane or rocket of the time could reach.

Laura would get the most attention if she was seen, having the highly sought blond hair and blue eyes, perfect for conceiving the Nazis' Aryan race. So Laura needed to remain hidden as much as possible. But in fact none of them wanted to be seen.

They had disassembled the stabilisation emitter so that each of them could carry parts and nobody needed a large rucksack, which would stand out. Resistance bombs were not uncommon in some parts of Nazi-controlled territory. They tried to carry as little as possible: a medical kit, the emitter and small firearms, along with flash-bangs and smoke grenades. Neither Thomas nor Laura had any intention of going into Nazi territory unarmed. They knew killing would be damaging to the space-time continuum, but that didn't mean they couldn't shoot someone in the leg if absolutely necessary.

They knew where they needed to reach, and it wasn't a great distance away, but the city was full of roadblocks and inspection points, not to mention patrolling soldiers. They needed to observe the patrol routes of the soldiers and look for any weaknesses that would allow to them to sneak by or through inspection points. If they engaged the soldiers and it went wrong, they could bring half an army down on the team, so they needed to move very cautiously. They used alleyways and rooftops and took advantage of guard shift changes to make slow progress. But eventually they came to a checkpoint they couldn't avoid or get around. Three armed guards were checking the identity documents of every driver and pedestrian.

"I'm not confident that we can deal with the three soldiers without a shot fired or alarm sounded," said Thomas.

"I agree," said Laura. "We need a distraction, something for them to focus on, while you sneak up behind them and take them out."

"A distraction would be ideal, but what?"

"I can distract them," said Laura, and she undressed a little to appear more alluring.

Thomas was a happily married man with two young children, but even he couldn't help but notice how attractive Laura looked.

Laura stepped out and slowly walked towards the soldiers, making suggestive gestures as she approached them. Meanwhile, Thomas circled around behind. Not noticing Thomas, two of the soldiers started to walk towards Laura, their intentions obvious. Laura could see Thomas's movements as two of the soldiers now had their backs to him. Thomas extended his baton and struck the remaining checkpoint solider hard, knocking him unconscious but without any audible sound. Not that it would have made a difference – the two other soldiers were far too distracted by Laura.

Thomas then moved stealthily up behind the soldiers, just as they were close to making inappropriate contact with Laura. Thomas signalled to Laura which one he would strike so she could hit the other at the same time. *Bang* – both were on the ground and no longer a threat. Laura took a sedative from the medical kit and injected a small dose into the soldiers to keep them asleep for a few hours.

It was slow going, but they eventually reached their destination. The rift was in front of them, and soldiers were posted in front of it. It looked like the Nazis were studying this rift, which was probably a good thing: studying meant they weren't taking action.

Clearly, Stephen and Laura couldn't set up the emitter on the ground, so they decided to place it on one of the rooftops. They couldn't leave it in the open, so they placed a small structure around it so that it looked like a roof shed.

Before they were finished, they heard a noise, a bit like an air raid siren but different. Thomas and Laura looked down on the streets and saw lots of soldiers moving around almost frantically. They were sure the sound was an alarm.

Stephen, meanwhile, noticed the temporal rift shimmer in a way that hadn't been observed before. He surmised that something was impacting the space-time continuum.

Thomas radioed Isaac to say that the emitter was in place and that they would be heading back and would need to be picked up. Stephen prompted Thomas to mention the unusual activity in the rift that he had observed. Then Thomas warned that it was likely they would be coming back with the Nazis close behind, so Isaac must be calm and prepared.

They tried to return the same way they had come, but they failed. As soon as the Nazis saw Laura and identified her as the woman from the earlier incident at the checkpoint, they began firing aggressively. The Nazi soldiers didn't show any indication of wanting to detain or question; they intended a permanent solution to their problem.

Stephen, having had no experience like it, simply tried to stay low, keep his head down and follow Thomas and Laura's lead. They stopped randomly to return fire, not trying to hit the Nazi soldiers but to slow or stop their advance. They could keep the Nazis behind them back with suppressing fire, but those ahead of them were a different problem. One advantage was the poor positioning of the Nazis: they were in front and behind and careless shots would go past Thomas, Laura and Stephen and hit their own men, so it wasn't a good ambush. Thomas and Laura had no choice but to shoot the soldiers in front of them – aiming to injure, not to kill.

They were close to *Hope* when Stephen was hit in the leg. He wouldn't be able to walk and he was bleeding badly. Laura took out the medical kit to quickly apply a bandage and slow the blood loss. Now the group couldn't escape together. They would all be shot and killed trying to carry Stephen to safety.

"I'm not going to make it, am I?" said Stephen.

"I don't think any of us are," Laura replied.

"Could you make it without me?"

"We aren't leaving you behind!"

"I'm dead either way," said Stephen, "so give me your weapon and anything you can spare, and I'll hold them back so you can escape."

"We aren't talking about this," said Thomas. "We don't leave people behind, and certainly not here."

"This isn't open for discussion," said Stephen. "I always wanted to be part of something bigger than myself, to make a difference. That's why I joined Project Salvation. Now give me the weapon and let my life mean something."

It was clear that Stephen was certain about his decision, and as much as they hated it, they honoured his wishes. Laura handed him her weapon along with extra magazines, and then kissed Stephen before rising and following Thomas towards *Hope*. Laura looked back only once to see Stephen firing and giving it everything he had, so much so that the Nazis were too occupied to dedicate many soldiers to go after Thomas and Laura.

The Nazis continued to pursue them until they reached *Hope*, and Isaac came out with an assault rifle to lay down covering fire until Thomas and Laura were aboard. A barrage of bullets was released as he was trying to get aboard himself, and one hit him in the shoulder. Isaac was knocked down to the ground by the bullet.

Thomas jumped out and crawled towards Isaac. He grabbed the rifle and returned fire. While the Nazis were taking cover, Laura ran out quickly to Isaac, put his arm around her neck and carried him back to *Hope*. Thomas kept his head down as he reloaded and the Nazi soldiers unleashed another barrage of fire, and then he began firing as he retreated.

Finally, all were aboard. Laura took ownership of the rifle and fired to keep the attackers back while Thomas got to the cockpit and started the engines. Then he flew them out of harm's way – at least for now.

Chapter 16: The Conflict of Two Times

While Thomas piloted *Hope*, Adhira and Laura tended to Isaac. Fortunately, the bullet hadn't hit bone or anything vital, but he was still bleeding and in pain. They gave him something for the pain, cauterized the wound, stitched it closed and then added a dressing and bandage. Shortly after they were done, Isaac passed out. He would need time to rest and recover, but time was running out and they still had two more emitters to set up.

They headed towards the other side of the Nazi region, towards the Roman Empire territory. As they approached the temporal rift between the two times, Thomas observed the rift shimmering in a way he hadn't seen before. It was just as Stephen had described. (Thomas hadn't noticed it before as he was far too focused on the Nazi soldiers and the situation ahead of him at the time.) He piloted *Hope* lower so that they could get a view of what was happening below.

Thomas called to Laura and Adhira to make sure his eyes weren't deceiving him or that tiredness wasn't causing his mind to play tricks. They all saw the same thing: arrows, spears and projectiles from a catapult directed at the Nazi soldiers. Roman warriors and Nazi soldiers were at war. The two must have been crossing between times, trying to expand their respective empires. The team were already expecting a challenge, being without Stephen and Isaac and going into a region under the control of the Roman Empire, but now it was a war zone too.

The Nazis would have better weapons and technology, plus greater numbers, but they couldn't commit all their resources and it was likely the Romans had struck first, given that the team had seen the Nazis studying the rift rather than walking through it. The Nazis could have suffered great losses and the Romans may now have some of their weapons. In close combat the Romans would win: they would be skilled with the sword and spear, whereas the Nazis were skilled with firearms. At this stage the tide of the battle was in the Romans' favour, but that would change: machine guns and tanks would devastate the Roman army.

"The Nazis were likely caught off guard, but the tide will soon turn in their favour," said Thomas.

"If they're crossing the rift and expanding their empire, won't it be the same on the other side?" said Adhira.

"Very likely if they're close to it," said Thomas.

"We must get to the rift as quickly as possible and see what challenge awaits us," said Laura.

After passing through the temporal rift, they searched for a quiet place, free from conflict. They found a spot that wasn't far from a town, but it appeared that nobody had discovered the rift yet, or their attention was focused elsewhere.

"Laura, I'll land close to the rift. Please get the emitter set up and then we'll hide it as best we can," said Thomas.

They both knew that the timer on the emitter wasn't the only concern here. If the Romans discovered them then they would be slaves at best, dead at worst. And if the Romans didn't find them, the Nazis would crush them under the tracks of their tanks. They had managed to hold their own in a small engagement with the Nazis, but a fully armed and equipped Nazi army would wipe them out. So would the Romans with enough soldiers, because Thomas and Laura would run out of ammunition well before the Romans ran out of soldiers.

Less than thirty-six hours remained on the emitter timers and they still had one more to place in the next time period. They had to do that and head back before the counter hit zero or they could be trapped in a dangerous past.

Thomas and Laura worked as quickly as they could while Adhira watched over Isaac and *Hope*. They set up and mostly buried the emitter so it would be very hard to spot – you would need to be very close to see it.

The blue of the rift was starting to fade and it was becoming easier to see the other side of the rift. It looked like the barriers between the times were fading away. It seemed fairly obvious that the warnings from the future were coming true. Thomas and Laura returned to *Hope* and they headed towards the last rift.

Chapter 17: Success or Failure

In the final time period, Thomas flew low to see if they were entering another war zone between people of two different time periods, the result of empire expansion. Curiously, he saw people on the ground, but nobody appeared to be moving. He asked Laura and Adhira to look to see if he was mistaken. The two women agreed: it didn't look like anyone or anything was moving.

While they were looking for signs of life and movement, Isaac awoke. He was groggy but slowly came back to his senses. He stumbled a little at first as he made his way to the cockpit.

"What are you all looking at?" he asked.

"You should be resting," said Adhira.

"I can rest once this is over," Isaac replied.

"It's what we can't see that's troubling us. Look down there – no movement of any kind that we can see," said Thomas.

"Then we need to go down and check for ourselves," said Isaac. "Find a remote spot within walking distance of a village and we can see if something unusual is happening here."

Once they landed, Isaac insisted on going to investigate. Adhira and Laura protested, as he was injured, but they couldn't talk him out of it.

Adhira said, "If you must go then I'm going with you. Doctor's orders."

"I'm going with you too," said Laura.

Their walking pace was slow so that Isaac didn't exert himself too much, but they arrived at the village before long. There were people and buildings, but they were all frozen in place. Some clothing looked like it was being blown in the wind but had been frozen in a single moment in time. They continued to explore the village and saw people frozen: with a cup in hand about to drink, about to take a bite of their bread. They went into different houses and from room to room. They saw a married couple together in their bedroom. Everywhere they went it was the same: everything frozen in a single moment in time.

"What could've caused this?" asked Isaac.

"I think it's the war between the Nazis and the Romans," said Adhira.

"Wait, say that again," said Isaac.

"The two armies were crossing the rift to go to war with each other. They were in the heat of battle when we left," said Laura.

"Now it makes sense, Alana from the future warned us if too many people cross into other times it would damage space-time continuum. We are seeing the results of that damage here; it has caused time to stop" said Isaac. "We must get back to *Hope* fast and do what we came here to do as quickly as possible."

They moved as quickly as they could, but unfortunately this opened up Isaac's stitches. Once back on *Hope*, Adhira redid Isaac's stitches and added a new dressing and bandage, while Thomas piloted *Hope* to their final destination. Laura had the emitter and was ready to go out and set up as soon as they landed. Isaac decided it was best for him to sit this one out; he had already opened his wound once today.

With time frozen in this region, nobody felt the need to hide or shelter the emitter, which was quite a time-saver. Once their work was done, they returned to their own time and place. They had around twenty-four hours before the timers hit zero, so a healthy leeway.

When they arrived in the present, Jessica was waiting for them. She had some bad news, but before that, she wanted to know what had happened and where Stephen was. Thomas briefly explained what had happened in Europe. After a moment's pause, Jessica began sharing her bad news. The changes seen in the other rifts had happened here too, and the residents were worried that they would soon be cut off from the past. Jessica had tried to reason with them, but a few of the residents had thought this was their last opportunity to get to the past before it was too late.

"We must go back to the past, find them and bring them back," said Isaac.

"How could we possibly find them and bring them back in less than a day?" asked Jessica.

"And those who've gone through might be only the first of many," said Laura.

"I'll speak to Michael and the other residents," said Isaac, "and show them the footage from the frozen time. Once they know that going back may result in their being frozen in time, their lives ending, I'm sure they'll reconsider."

"We still have the problem of finding those people in the past, though. We have no idea how to do it," said Adhira.

"It's a long shot, but we can ask the computer on *Hope*. Maybe there's some way to detect them or identify them," said Jessica.

"I can't think of a better alternative," said Isaac.

The computer confirmed that travelling through a temporal rift would leave a trace. The time travellers' bodies would be imbued with temporal energy. Given their work on Project Salvation, the team already had equipment for measuring and detecting this type of energy. With a few modifications to *Hope*, they could scan the ground below for anyone saturated with this energy. There were two problems: it would take a few hours to make the adjustments to *Hope*, and once they found a person, they would need help to identify them. Given how many times Jessica and the others had crossed through the various rifts, their bodies were saturated, so the handheld instruments wouldn't be accurate if one of them was there doing the testing. They would need the help of the police officers of the time to check the individuals and arrest them, and then they could be collected and returned to their own time.

Although the police had only known Isaac and Laura up to this point, the team decided that Jessica was best suited for this mission given her experiences with the Hopi and Aboriginals and her scientific skills.

They crossed through to the 1980s, and Laura introduced Jessica, who quickly gained the trust of the police officers. Jessica showed the officers the footage from the place where time was frozen, so that they knew how important it was that they were successful.

Thomas would pilot *Hope* while Jessica used the equipment to locate the few people who had journeyed back to this past time. The search radius was limited to around a quarter of a mile, but knowing the direction and monitoring the movements of the visitors from their own time, they could do a quick test for anyone who was suspected until they found their person.

Eventually, all the residents of the present had been arrested and were waiting for the team near the rift. Once everyone was aboard *Hope*, it was time to return home. But just as they approached, the emitter was activated. They didn't know how long it would take for the repair to complete or the consequences of flying through during the repair, but they had little choice. They accelerated as quickly as possible to make it through the rift, and then shortly after they were through, it faded away.

Chapter 18: The Choice

Back in the present, Thomas landed *Hope* to allow the village residents to disembark, and then he and Jessica waited for Isaac, Adhira and Laura to join them. Michael followed close behind, seeking answers.

"We have no idea whether we've been successful yet. We'll be leaving now to find that answer," Isaac told Michael.

The Project Salvation team circled the globe in space, looking for temporal rifts or energy. The rifts were all gone and they couldn't detect any sign of temporal energy. It was as if the last experiment had never happened.

Then the voice of Alana came from the computer: "I have a recorded message from Alana which was set to be delivered if it was confirmed that you were successful in your mission. And you were successful: you have repaired the damage to the space-time continuum and saved everyone in the past, present and future.

"But you must be asking yourselves, what's next? Aren't we back to exactly the same point where we started? Nothing has changed and you're still on the same path to a devastating future. You have a decision to make which could alter your future. We can't know for certain; only you can discover that.

"Even in your future, my present, we still don't know how to safely time travel. We did, however, discover a way to repair the damage done by the past generations. Unfortunately, it came too late. The population had been reduced to such a level that we didn't have enough genetic diversity to rebuild the human race. You, on the other hand, have the option to use our technology and save the world.

"But to do so will create a temporal paradox and we can't know the result of that. It could unravel the space-time continuum just as badly as your previous experiment. Or it could split your future into a parallel reality, so both the old and new futures exist. Or these two realities could merge into a culmination of both.

"Alternatively, you can send this craft into the sun, along with the data, and continue to decide your own future. Whichever decision you make, this craft must be destroyed so that future technology isn't misused.

"You now have a choice to make. Once you have decided, tell the computer and it will enact your wishes. Whatever you decide, all people throughout time owe you a debt of thanks."

"I'm not qualified or suited to make this decision. I'll leave it to the rest of you," said Isaac.

"After all we went through to fix our mistake and save the world, you're going to walk away now?" said Jessica.

"My mistake led us to that point in the beginning," Isaac said. "I needed to own my mistake and make sure nobody suffered for it. But if this journey has taught me anything, it's that I'm as much a part of the problem as those who doomed the world in the first place. If we'd listened to others like the Hopi and led a different life, then we would never have needed saving. I'd like to leave this decision to you and Adhira. You have heart and have become so much more than who you were at the beginning. I believe you're best placed to decide the future."

"Thomas and Laura, what do you think?" asked Jessica.

"I've done my part and saved my family," said Thomas. "Now I just want to go home to them and leave this choice to those with the wisdom to make it."

"I've never really made any choices in my life," said Laura. "I went into the services because my family had a history of national service; I simply followed in their footsteps. The more I look at my life, the more I realise that others have made my decisions for me. So I don't think I should have a say in this choice."

"As a scientist," said Jessica, "I want to explore the unknown. But if we simply fix the problem, will anyone have learnt anything?"

"Nobody will have the chance to learn anything if we do nothing," said Adhira.

"What if we wait – share our story so that the world can learn from our journey, as we did? Then, when the time is right and we're ready as a race, we use the future technology to give us one more chance," said Jessica.

They all agreed on this. After taking the information they needed from the computer's memory, they sent *Hope* into the sun.

When they returned to the Project Salvation research facility, they were greeted by government officials desperate to know the results of the latest test. It was like the last two weeks had never happened.

"There's much to tell you," said Isaac, "but not just you select few. It's a story for the world to hear and learn from."

The story was printed and shared, with a few omissions, under the title *How the World, Past, Present and Future, Almost Ended*.

After a few years, most people had read the book and it had been discussed in many public forums. Once the lessons were learned, the truth of the ending was revealed.

Jessica and Isaac had been working together in secret to prepare for the day when people would be ready for that second chance. They flipped the switch and made the announcement, and then waited to see which possibility would be their reality. It took time to be certain, but they found that they had created an alternate reality. Their lives had hope, made possible by the reality which had none.

Made in the USA
Columbia, SC
19 November 2020